Date: 10/27/22

**PALM BEACH COUNTY
LIBRARY SYSTEM**

**3650 Summit Boulevard
West Palm Beach, FL 33406**

Health and My Body

Bullying

by Martha E. H. Rustad

PEBBLE
a capstone imprint

Pebble Explore is published by Pebble, an imprint of Capstone
1710 Roe Crest Drive
North Mankato, Minnesota 56003
www.capstonepub.com

Library of Congress Cataloging-in-Publication Data
Names: Rustad, Martha E. H. (Martha Elizabeth Hillman), 1975- author.
Title: Bullying / Martha E. H. Rustad.
Description: North Mankato : Capstone Press, 2021. | Series: Health and my body | Includes bibliographical references and index. | Audience: Ages 6-8 | Audience: Grades 2-3 | Summary: "Teasing. Spreading rumors. Leaving someone out on purpose. These are types of bullying, and bullying is never OK. You have the power to stop bullying by using respect and kindness, and it's an important power to have"— Provided by publisher.
Identifiers: LCCN 2020027224 (print) | LCCN 2020027225 (ebook) | ISBN 9781977132161 (hardcover) | ISBN 9781977133182 (paperback) | ISBN 9781977153920 (pdf)
Subjects: LCSH: Bullying—Juvenile literature. | Cyberbullying—Juvenile literature. | Bullying—Prevention—Juvenile literature.
Classification: LCC BF637.B85 R87 2021 (print) | LCC BF637.B85 (ebook) | DDC 302.34/3—dc23
LC record available at https://lccn.loc.gov/2020027224
LC ebook record available at https://lccn.loc.gov/2020027225

Image Credits
Dreamstime: Akulamatiau, 27; Susan Sheldon, 16; iStockphoto: LSOphoto, 20; monkeybusinessimages, 18; Shutterstock: Antonio Guillem, 23; ChameleonsEye, 11; Creativa Images, 26; Daisy Daisy, 6; Dawn Shearer-Simonetti, 13; Lopolo, cover, 19; Monkey Business Images, 12, 25, 29; photonova, design element throughout; Rawpixel.com, 15; Suzanne Tucker, 21; Tero Vesalainen, 10; Twin Design, 7; Veja, 9; wavebreakmedia, 5

Editorial Credits
Editor: Christianne Jones; Designer: Sarah Bennett; Media Researcher: Morgan Walters; Production Specialist: Laura Manthe

Table of Contents

Bold words are in the glossary.

What Is Bullying?

People don't always get along. People fight. They say mean things. It is normal and healthy. It is a part of life everyone experiences. But bullying is different.

Bullying is picking on someone over and over. It is using power to make a person do something or feel a certain way. Bullying is making yourself feel good by making someone else feel bad. Bullying is never OK.

People bully others for many
reasons. Some do it to try to be more
popular. They think it will make people
like them. Bullying makes them feel
important.

Others copy what they see. They might bully people because they get bullied by someone else.

People bully because they like to be in charge. Bullying uses fear to control others.

Kinds of Bullying

There are three kinds of bullying. The first kind is **physical**. It can be hitting or kicking. It can be tripping or pulling hair. Physical bullying can also be breaking someone else's things.

Every day, Joe plays on his swing after school. But when his neighbor comes over, she pushes him off. She wants the swing for herself. She is using physical bullying.

The second kind of bullying is **verbal**. It hurts people's feelings. It can be calling names or teasing. It can be threats or mean words. Verbal bullying includes mean words written on paper, in texts, in email, or on social media.

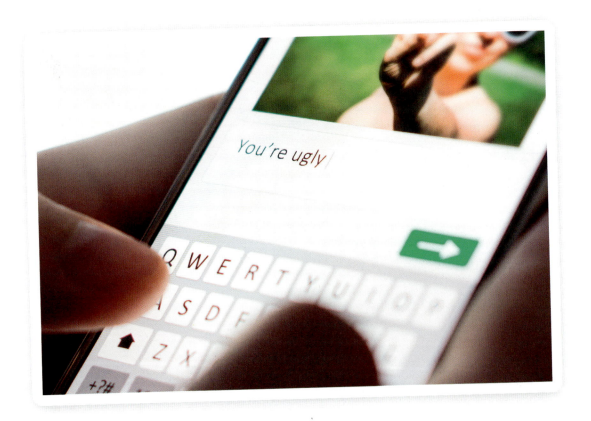

Ari loved to play with dolls. But Mel called her a baby for still playing with dolls. Now Ari doesn't play with her favorite thing anymore. Mel is using verbal bullying.

The third kind of bullying is **social**. It can change what other people think. This includes leaving someone out. It can also be spreading **rumors**. It can happen in person or online.

Lu shared a secret with Paul. Paul told everyone in the class. Now Lu feels sad and embarrassed. Paul is using social bullying.

What You Can Do

What should you do if someone is bullying you? It is OK to feel scared. But you can make a plan. Think of what you can say or do before it happens.

If someone says something mean to you, use words to get them to stop. Use a strong voice. Tell them how their actions make you feel. Ask them to leave you alone.

Stick up for yourself. Stand tall. Act brave even if you don't feel brave.

One way to work against bullying is to avoid it. Stay with a friend or a group of friends. Play near adults. Bullying often takes place when kids are away from adults.

Try to ignore bullying words. Some people use bullying to get a **reaction**. You could pretend not to hear them. Some kids think of something funny to say in return. Jokes sometimes stop bullying from continuing.

You might see a friend being bullied. You might feel scared for them. You might feel scared for yourself. So what should you do?

Tell someone who is bullying to back down. You can tell an adult. Adults can always help you deal with bullying.

Be kind to any kids who are bullied. Sit by them on the bus or at lunch. If you see someone sitting alone, ask them to join you. Make new friends!

What should you do if someone bullies you physically? This might be tripping or pushing. It is not a good idea to hit back. Even if you feel mad, hitting is never OK.

If you feel unsafe, walk away. Find help. Tell a trusted adult. Adults need to know about bullying behavior.

You can work against all kinds of bullying. Do not put up with it. It is not healthy for anyone.

Online Bullying

Online bullying can take place on social media. It can happen in texts or in emails. People might send messages you don't want. People can easily spread rumors on social media. They can say mean things or call people names.

You can work against online bullying. Tell an adult if you see online bullying. Some sites have tools to report mean comments or bullying.

Be sure to stay safe online. Keep your password secret. You don't want anyone using your account. Also, check your **privacy** settings. Ask an adult to help you stay private online.

Be careful what photos you post. Photos can be easily shared with people. It is not OK for anyone to post photos of you without your permission.

Think about what you post on social media. Be kind. Choose to say nice words online. Remember that your words can be shared with everyone. Words and photos last forever online.

If you see something online that makes you feel bad, talk to an adult. Everyone deserves to feel safe online.

Be Kind

Bullying uses fear to lead. Good leaders lead with good ideas, not fear. Practice being a good leader. Act kindly. Encourage others to be kind as well. Make everyone feel safe. Let everyone have a chance to talk.

If you feel like being mean, take a break. Walk away if you need to. Stop and think before you talk. Use words to help people feel better, not worse.

Not everyone will be nice. But remember that everyone has struggles. Everyone deserves **respect**. Try to include everyone and always be kind. And no matter what, bullying is never OK.

Glossary

physical (FIZ-uh-kuhl)—having to do with your body

popular (POP-yuh-lur)—liked or enjoyed by many people

privacy (PRYE-vi-see)—the ability to keep something to yourself and not share it

reaction (ree-AK-shuhn)—the way you act toward something that happens

respect (ri-SPEKT)—the belief in the quality and worth of others and yourself

rumor (ROO-mur)—a story that is spread by word of mouth but that may not be true

social (SOH-shuhl)—about relationships with other people

verbal (VUR-buhl)—having to do with words

Read More

Miller, Connie Colwell. *You Can Stop Bullying: Stand By or Stand Up?* Mankato, MN: Amicus Ink, 2020.

Olson, Elsie. *Be Kind!: A Hero's Guide to Beating Bullying.* Minneapolis: Abdo, 2020.

Spilsbury, Louise. *Questions and Feelings About Bullying.* North Mankato, MN: Picture Window Books, 2020.

Internet Sites

About Bullying and Cyberbullying
www.stompoutbullying.org/get-help/about-bullying-and-cyberbullying

BrainPOP Jr.: Bullying
jr.brainpop.com/health/besafe/bullying

Dealing with Bullies
www.kidshealth.org/en/kids/bullies.html

Index